Fantastic Folk Tales

The Tailor at the Haunted Church

Scottish Folk Tale

An imprint of Om Books International

One fine day, the great MacDonald was sitting in his castle at Saddell, Scotland. He decided that he will get a pair of trews (traditional pair of trousers) tailored for himself for the upcoming King's ball.

However, MacDonald decided that he would test the courage of the tailor who would sew the trews for him. He told his men to announce in the city that he would give huge rewards to the tailor who could sew him a pair of trews by night at the old church.

It was believed that the old church was haunted. Now, most of the tailors in town heard the announcement and were scared and whispered, "What will we do with all that reward if the ghost eats us up at night?"

Even though the reward money was tempting to many, they were too scared to accept the challenge.

But there was one young, clever tailor who was not scared of the ghost. In fact, he was curious to see one. As the reward money was tempting, the tailor arrived at the castle to accept MacDonald's challenge.

"Are you not scared of the ghost at the old church, young man?" MacDonald asked the tailor. The tailor replied, "You will have your trews by the morning, Sir. And for the ghost, I can deal with it." MacDonald was impressed with the tailor's courage.

Armed with his tools and cloth, the tailor reached the old church by nightfall. He swiftly chose a gravestone and lighting up a candle, began working on the trews. Suddenly, the ground shook beneath his feet, but he continued to sew.

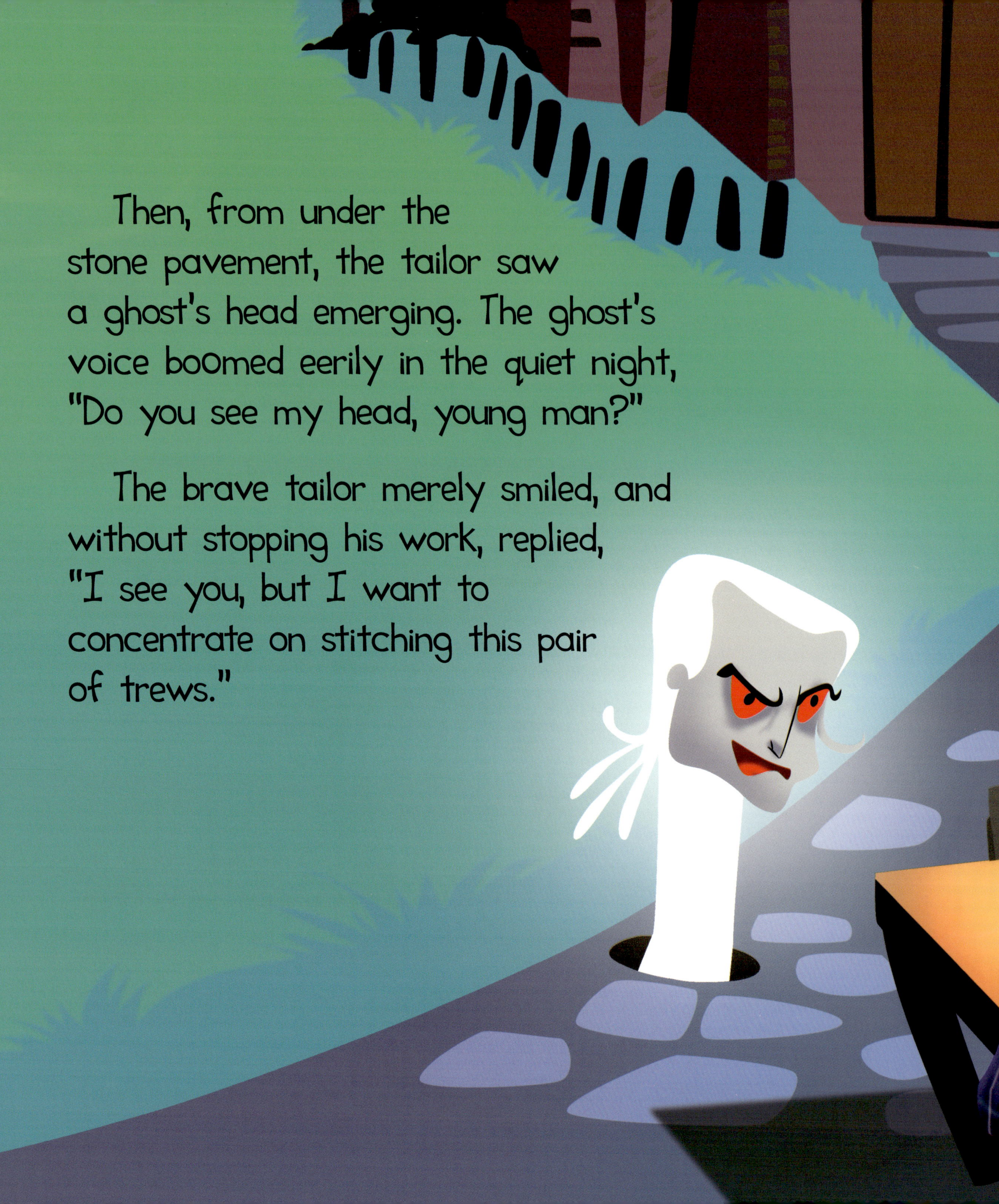

Then, from under the stone pavement, the tailor saw a ghost's head emerging. The ghost's voice boomed eerily in the quiet night, "Do you see my head, young man?"

The brave tailor merely smiled, and without stopping his work, replied, "I see you, but I want to concentrate on stitching this pair of trews."

The ghost looked surprised. He stared at the tailor with burning red eyes and slowly rose out of the ground till his neck could be seen.

"Do you see this long neck of mine?" the ghost asked. Once again, the tailor smiled and replied, "I see you, but I want to concentrate on stitching this pair of trews."

The ghost grew angrier with the tailor. He thought, *How can this man ignore me? Do I not scare him? I shall teach him a lesson.* He pushed himself from the ground further, till his massive chest and long arms could be seen. The tailor realised that if he keeps avoiding the ghost, he will come out and kill him.

He thought of an idea and started making long stitches in the trews, furiously fast. "Can you see my huge chest?" bellowed the ghost. The tailor calmly replied, "I see you, but I want to concentrate on stitching this pair of trews."

The ghost was very angry and stepped out from the pavement. When the tailor saw the long, pale legs of the ghost emerge, he understood that he will have to run for his life! He had finished stitching by now. He grabbed the trews and made a dash towards the castle. The ghost screamed at the tailor, "You teased me too much and now you shall be punished for it. Wait till I catch you!"

As soon as the tailor got inside the castle, he shut the gate. The ghost crashed against the gate, but was unable to get inside. He hit the wall near the gate with his hand and left a mark of his five fingers, which can still be seen today. The relieved tailor went to MacDonald and handed him the trews.

MacDonald was very impressed with the trews and the tailor's courage. True to his promise, he gave a handsome reward to the tailor, who walked away happily. But till now MacDonald has failed to see the long stitches on his favourite pair of trews!